Fireworks!

Written by Mara Conlon

Illustrated by Paige Billin-Frye

Grosset & Dunlap
New York

ISBN 0-448-42587-4   A B C D E F G H I J

"Rise and shine, sleepyheads! It's time to get up for day camp! And don't forget about tonight!" Dad told Jenna and Matty.

"I bet you can't wait for tonight, huh Mom?" Jenna said.
"Jenna, you know how I hate those loud noises. They hurt my ears. Only your dad will be taking you girls tonight," said her mom.

"What's tonight, Jenna?" Matty asked her big sister.
"We're going to the waterfront. You know, bang-bang-boom!"

"Oh yeah. I knew that", said Matty. She wanted her big sister to think she was cool. But the truth was, Matty didn't know what Jenna was talking about at all!

What was going to happen at the waterfront tonight? Matty thought.

"I hope day camp goes fast today. I can't wait for tonight!" Jenna said, eagerly waving.
"Me too," said Matty quietly.

Matty sat at the picnic table and thought, "How can I find out what's going on tonight?"

At lunch, all the kids were talking about the big night.
"My favorite ones are the red ones," said Jenna.
"I like the ones that start out white and then turn into blue," said Stacey.

Matty was still very confused. She heard someone say, "The squiggly ones are the best!" Matty thought to herself, "What in the world could be loud, red or blue, and squiggly?"

When Jenna, Matty, and their dad arrived at the waterfront, there were lots of people there! They searched for a good spot to sit down.

"Jenna," Matty whispered shyly, "I don't *really* know what's gonna happen tonight."

Jenna smiled. "How could I forget? This is your first time seeing fireworks!" said Jenna. "Just wait and see . . ."

Then all of a sudden . . . bang—zoom—boom! Up in the sky there were blue ones, red ones, squiggly ones, purple ones, star ones, and lots more!

Matty stared up at the colorful sky. "Wow!" she said, smiling, "I love fireworks!"